The Monster of Shiversands Cove

First published 2015 by
A & C Black, an imprint of Bloomsbury Publishing Plc
50 Bedford Square,
London, WC1B 3DP

www.bloomsbury.com

Bloomsbury is a registered trademark of Bloomsbury Publishing Plc

A CIP catalogue for this book is available from the British Library

ISBN: 978-1-4729-0741-7

Printed and bound by CPI Group (UK) Ltd, Croydon CR0 4YY

1 3 5 7 9 10 8 6 4 2

The Monster of Shiversands Cove

EMMA FISCHEL

Illustrated by
Peter Cottrill

A & C BLACK
AN IMPRINT OF BLOOMSBURY
LONDON OXFORD NEW YORK NEW DELHI SYDNEY

Contents

Chapter One
Shiversands Cove

'This holiday is doomed,' I said. 'Because Rory should be on this holiday but Rory is *not.*'

I glared at the back of Dad's head. Then, I glared out of the car window. I glared at the road, winding along, far above the sea.

Rory is my very best friend. I was three when I met him. He moved into my street and I spotted him straight away: as soon as he clambered out of his car seat, clutching a big green lollipop.

Rory spotted me too. He came skipping over, beaming, offered me a lick of the lollipop and that was it. I was Rory's best friend from then on and he was mine.

The mums and dads became best friends, too. So for the last four years we have all had holidays together.

But not this year.

'I was expecting this holiday to be brilliant, just like the last four,' I grumbled at the back of Dad's head. 'But it will *not* be. Because Rory's mum and dad have *ruined* things.'

First, they both got new jobs, two hundred miles away from their old jobs. So, one month and three days ago, Rory had to move.

Second, moving costs a lot, so Rory's mum and dad decided there would be no holiday this year. And they cancelled it.

'Cheer up, Stan,' said Dad. 'We'll still have a good time.'

'I doubt it,' I said gloomily. 'Not with no Rory. Just Magnus.'

I turned and glared at Magnus.

Magnus, my brother, is four years old and he's short and stout, with bobbing golden curls. He was lolling in his car seat next to me, fast asleep, dribbling, twitching and muttering. His big fairy-spotting guide was lying open on his lap.

'The *whole* first hour of this journey,' I said to the back of Dad's head, 'I had to listen to Magnus telling me about his magic eyes.'

Yes. Magic eyes.

Magic eyes, so Magnus told me, are something all little kids have. Special eyes: eyes that can see fairies, and elves, and little pixies, and all sorts. Magnus also told me that a little kid who *does* see a fairy, or whatever, will keep hold of those magic eyes and be able to see fairies forever and *ever*. Even as a grown-up . . .

As if!

'The *second* hour,' I said, 'I had to listen to Magnus telling me *all* his fairy-hunting plans for this holiday.'

On and on and *on* Magnus went and I could *not* shut him up. Even when I stuck my headphones on, he kept pulling them off to chat more.

'The *third* hour,' I said, 'Magnus showed me pictures in his fairy-spotting guide. And he spent fifteen whole minutes explaining, *not* that I wanted to know, how seaside fairies have special waterproof wings so that they can splash and play in the waves without their wings getting waterlogged. And now, Magnus is *finally* asleep but, judging by all the dribbling and muttering, he is *dreaming* about fairies!'

I slumped down in my seat, glum as anything.

'Almost there,' Dad said cheerily. Then, the car slowed down and turned left, down a very narrow lane, winding towards the sea.

The sea got closer and closer and then, right below us, I could see it.

Shiversands Cove.

It was small and sandy, with big black rocks at both ends, and jagged cliffs stretching up and away above them. There were cottages, two of them, clinging to the slope behind the beach: a pale blue cottage at the far end and right ahead of us, a white one.

Shiversands Cottage. Our holiday home.

★ ★ ★

Shiversands Cottage was old and crooked. It was leaning a bit to one side and all painted white, with a black wooden frame. It had lots of little windows with diamond-shaped panes.

I got out of the car and stood with Dad. He stretched and looked around, then gave a big happy sniff. 'Sea air,' he said. 'A beach. Cliffs.'

Then he pointed out to sea, to a small island, linked by a rickety bridge from the edge of our cove. 'And look,' he said, 'there. An island to explore. Perfect!'

Dad was right. It *was* perfect. But that made me feel even more glum, because it was perfect, except for one thing.

No Rory.

So I glared at the pale blue cottage at the far end of the cove. The one Rory should be staying in, but wasn't.

'We had plans for this holiday,' I said. 'Big plans.' Which we did: digging plans, snorkelling plans, all sorts of plans.

'And if Rory were here, then Amy would be too,' I said. 'So Magnus could do all his fairy chat with Amy, instead of me.'

Amy is Rory's sister: another four-year-old fairy fanatic.

I felt my shoulders droop. 'And Rory said we could train Bagel to do the high jump this holiday,' I said. 'But *now*, instead of Rory and his dog, I am stuck with Magnus and his hamster. And the hamster is an idiot, and it bites. So . . .'

I blinked. There was something out there, far out at sea, swimming behind the island.

I tugged on Dad's sleeve. 'Dad,' I said. 'What's that?'

Dad looked. 'What's what?' he said.

'It's gone now, behind the island,' I said. 'But there was something there, something big, something greeny-grey.'

Just then, I heard a gasp from the car seat and a small piping voice.

'Daddy, Stan,' it said. 'I am *absolutely* ready to go fairy hunting!'

Magnus was awake: beaming out of the car window and struggling with the straps of his car seat. 'Stan, help me, help me,' he said. 'Get me out!'

I opened the car door and undid the straps. Magnus scrambled out, eyes all shiny as he stared at the sea. He clasped his hands together. 'Oh, I do hope I find a fairy! And if I do find a fairy, I must let Fairy Fenella know!'

I groaned; I just couldn't help it. Not Fairy Fenella. *Again.* I heard a *lot* about Fairy Fenella in the car: too much, in fact.

'Magnus,' I snapped. 'Fairy Fenella is *not* a real fairy.'

Magnus just tittered and patted my hand. 'Stan,' he said, 'you are such a silly. Fairy Fenella *is* a real fairy.'

'She is *not*,' I said. 'She's . . .'

'*Stan*,' said Dad.

Dad can get a lot of meaning into a 'Stan', and this 'Stan' was a warning. Say any more about Fairy Fenella being some grown-up idiot who thinks it's funny to prance around on TV, filling little kids' heads with nonsense about day-to-day life as a fairy, and magic eyes, and all that stuff, and you are in Big Trouble.

Even though it was the truth.

★ ★ ★

Inside, Shiversands Cottage was all higgledy-piggledy: full of sloping floors and small dark rooms filled with big dark shadows. It was very old, very dark and a bit spooky. Which I liked.

The sitting room was darkest and spookiest of all. I pushed open the door and walked in. It had two narrow windows, a sloping floor and two saggy old sofas. There were shelves crammed full of old books, and pictures everywhere: old black and white photos of stormy seas, of huge waves crashing over big black rocks, and of olden days people in olden days clothes, standing by olden days boats.

Over the fireplace was a big dark painting. It was some kind of sea monster, rearing up over a boat at night. An ugly sort of sea monster, looming out of the waves and the gloom. Its head was arched back, its eyes were popping, and its snout was open, as though it was roaring.

Excellent!

Up the narrow, creaking stairs there were three rooms: a bathroom and two bedrooms. The one straight ahead had a nameplate on the door, which said:

CAPTAIN'S CABIN

Then, there were three small steps up to another room, with a sign, which said:

CREW'S CABIN

Crew's cabin was small but cosy. It had two beds, one for me and one for Magnus, with a big porthole-shaped window between them. I stared out of it and down the long, sloping back garden. It had a fence at the bottom with a gate on to the rocks above the cove, and the sand, and the sea.

The sea was flat and calm in the cove; not a breath of wind was ruffling the water. Further out at sea, the sun was dropping behind the island, a red setting sun.

I blinked.

Huge ripples were coming in from the sea, rippling into the cove and widening in circles across it.

As if, well . . . as if there were a big fish somewhere out there: a *very* big fish indeed.

Chapter Two
Princess Splishy-Splashy

Next morning, the sun woke me, glinting in through a chink in the curtains. I sat up and looked out of the porthole. It was a bright sunny day and the sea was all sparkly. Then, just behind the island, out at sea:

WHOOSH!

All of a sudden, a huge jet of water, like a giant fountain, shot right up in the air.

I leaned forward and clutched the edge of the porthole. Now *that* was interesting. I knew what it was straight away: a waterspout. And where there was a waterspout that size, there was a *whale*. There had to be. I stared hard. Brilliant! A whale, right out there, behind the island.

Now, I am the number-one fan of whales, because whales are extremely interesting creatures. Not even fish, for a start, even though they swim in the sea. No, whales are mammals, long-living mammals. Some whales, especially the ones that swim about in the Arctic Ocean, can live to over one hundred and fifty years old. And whales are musical mammals, too. They like inventing tunes. Whales swim about, singing their tunes and when they get bored with singing one tune, which whales do in the end, they just invent a new one.

Then, there are the waterspouts. All whales make waterspouts. A whale shoots water out of a blowhole, sometimes even two, on the top of its head, and that helps it breathe in the water.

Dolphins and porpoises do waterspouts, too. But that waterspout was much too big to be a dolphin or porpoise. It was a whale. It had to be. And a whale expert could tell what sort of whale that was, just from the shape of the waterspout, but I couldn't. I had no idea what sort of whale it was.

All the same, the whale was a good start to the day. Then the day got better because Dad and Magnus woke up and, once Magnus had his water wings on, we all ran down the garden and across the beach, and swam before breakfast.

We splashed about and chucked a beach ball around. Then, I did a bit of snorkelling around the rocks at the side while Dad helped Magnus with his swimming strokes.

After that, Dad cooked a big breakfast: piles of pancakes and toast and bacon. We ate outside, at a table on the patio, with the cove glinting and sparkling in front of us.

Then, we made a find: a shed full of interesting stuff at the bottom of the garden. There was a big folded bit of fishing net, the strong kind that fishing boats drag behind them, and there were coils of rope and tins with weird names on them like 'Bloodworms', which Dad said were fishing bait. There were also some old magazines and old flowerpots, beach balls, a Frisbee and a cricket set.

I was starting to feel that maybe this holiday wasn't doomed, that maybe it would be good, when we heard the sound of a car coming down the lane. A car loaded up with holiday stuff, and heading straight for the pale blue cottage.

The car stopped and the doors opened. A mum got out, and a dad. And . . .

Oh no.

A girl. She was Magnus-sized, and was wearing a sticky-out princess dress, a tiara, and small stout shoes. She came thudding straight out of the car and down to the beach, bellowing, 'Princess Splishy-Splashy! Where are you? It's me, Claudia. I'm back!'

She stood there bellowing for at least two minutes, and for someone so short, she had a very big bellow. Then, she folded her arms, turned, spotted me and Magnus in our garden, and came stomping over, frowning.

'Have *you* seen Princess Splishy-Splashy?' she said.

★ ★ ★

Princess Splishy-Splashy turned out to be a mermaid.

Yes, a *mermaid*. A mermaid which the bellower, Claudia, said she met last year. Because last year, Claudia stayed in our cottage and every day, so Claudia said, Princess Splishy-Splashy sat on the rocks out on the island, singing and combing her long golden hair. Sometimes she would even dive into the water and swim about with Claudia.

'I was expecting her to be there now,' Claudia said. 'I had plans for us.' Then her eyebrows knotted together. 'Hm. I wonder where she's gone?'

I gaped at her. What a strange child. Why invent a mermaid and then pretend she had gone missing? I had three imaginary friends when I was a little kid, all goblins. But I *never* pretended my goblins went missing. I pretended they had chicken pox. I pretended they spat out their greens and hated brushing their teeth. But I *never* pretended my goblins went missing. What was the point?

Magnus did *not* seem to find Claudia strange, not at all. He stared at her, thrilled and she stared at him.

'You,' Claudia said, 'are being my holiday friend.' Then, she grabbed Magnus by the hand and dragged him off, while Dad got busy chatting to Claudia's mum and dad, making himself some grown-ups friends for the holiday.

Which was why it was only me who saw it.

It was a glimpse: just a quick glimpse, out of the corner of my eye. A glimpse of something leaping out of the water, just behind the island. Something huge and greeny-grey, twirling around so fast it was a blur. Then, it dived and was gone.

Chapter Three
Fairies and Monsters

I spent a *lot* of that day digging, and digging is something I usually enjoy. But not today, because today digging reminded me of Rory and of all the digging we did, every holiday for the past four years.

We had big digging plans for this year. We both drew designs for our digging: nine of them between us.

Then Rory's mum and dad cancelled the holiday.

I was digging one of our designs now, our castle design. But digging a castle alone was not half as much fun as digging a castle with Rory.

Still, I dug on. Digging – and watching out for the whale. I was hoping I'd see it again, leaping out of the water, and get a clearer look at it. I didn't, though. So I dug on, trying and trying not to think how much better it would be if Rory were here, digging too.

Trying and failing, feeling glummer and glummer by the minute. But the glummer I got, the harder I dug. So, in the end, the castle was done. Finished.

It was a work of genius, utter genius. It stretched out across the beach, with lots of turrets and battlements, and even a small cobbled courtyard and a traitors' gate.

I stood back, admiring it. I was planning to take a picture of it and send it to Rory. Then, I heard a bellow from the far end of the beach. The bellow of a four-year-old fairy hunter: Claudia.

'There's one,' Claudia bellowed.

I turned.

Claudia was pointing one small fat finger straight past me and behind her Magnus started shrieking. 'A fairy!' he shrieked, clasping his hands. 'A fairy!'

I gaped, as the two of them started thudding across the sand, eyes shining, cheeks pink, both huffing, both puffing, both holding out fishing nets. Closer and closer and closer they came thudding.

'Watch out!' I yelled.

Too late.

They thudded straight through my castle. They destroyed the whole thing.

I yelled at them. I yelled at them for quite a long time.

They stood there, eyes popping as they listened to me yelling. When I stopped, Magnus clutched my arm, eyes shining. 'But Stan,' he said, 'we couldn't help it. We saw a fairy!' Then he clasped his hands together. 'And now, I will *keep* my magic eyes! I will see fairies forever!'

Enough. *Enough*! I looked down at the shattered remains of my brilliant castle and kicked my foot, fed up and furious.

'There is NO SUCH THING as magic eyes ... or fairies,' I yelled, right in Magnus's face. 'But there IS such a thing as stupid little four-year-olds who should LOOK where they ARE GOING!'

Claudia stepped in front of me and glared up at me. She wagged her finger. 'You should *not* shout at little children,' she said, hands on hips.

Then, she grabbed Magnus by the arm. 'Come on, Magnus,' she said, 'we are going *to tame* that fairy. We'll have a tea party for it.'

She turned, stuck her nose in the air and glared at me again. 'And *you* are not invited,' she said, as she dragged Magnus off.

★ ★ ★

That night, Magnus was sitting up in bed, staring at his fairy-spotting guide. One small finger slowly moving across the page, his mouth making word shapes.

Magnus can't actually read. Not properly, not yet but, then, he doesn't need to. He knows his fairy-spotting guide off by heart. Mum or Dad read it to him most nights.

He snapped the book shut when he saw me and beamed.

'Stan,' he said. 'Isn't this a lovely holiday? When I was with Claudia today, we *did* find a fairy! We did! At last!'

Now, Magnus propped himself up on his pillow, beaming even more. 'We are calling our fairy Harry,' he said. 'And Claudia says that two lovely little children like us will definitely be able to tame Harry.'

I got into bed, hoping Magnus would shut up soon.

He didn't.

'Claudia says that when we tame Harry, we can *share* Harry,' he said. 'And Harry can sleep one night at her holiday home, then one night here.'

I felt my teeth beginning to grind but Magnus hadn't finished.

'And we can do a drawing of Harry,' he said. 'Because, Stan, we can't take a picture of Harry. Fairies get very upset if little children take pictures of them. Fairies don't like it. Fairies get scared when the light flashes in their faces. Fairy Fenella says.'

I felt my teeth grind more but Magnus *still* hadn't finished.

'And when we do the drawing we are going to send it to Fairy Fenella and get a Fairy Fenella badge,' he said proudly. 'Because, Stan, Fairy Fenella gives lovely badges to children who send her things. Claudia already has a bronze Fairy Fenella badge for making a tiny handbag out of felt and glue, for a fairy. So this time, Claudia might get a *silver* Fairy Fenella badge. And if this is a magic hotspot – because Fairy Fenella says there *are* magic hotspots, Stan, special places where magic is extra strong – we might find more fairies. Or even some little elves . . .'

Now, this was the point where I snapped. I could *not* help it. Magnus was going on and on and *on*. And there I was, stuck listening with no Rory and no friends my own age. Just two weeks of listening to Magnus. *And* Claudia.

'If this *is* a magic hotspot,' I snapped, 'there won't just be fairies or mermaids or elves, there'll be a monsters too.'

I know. I *know*. It was mean but I just could *not* help it.

Magnus looked at me and tittered. 'Stan, you're being a silly again,' he said, wagging his finger. 'There are *no* monsters. Monsters lived in the olden days. They're all gone now. Fairy Fenella said.'

'Fairy Fenella is *lying*,' I said. 'She doesn't want to scare you. There are monsters, loads of them. Human monsters, like Medusa.'

'Medusa?' said Magnus, eyes popping.

'A lady monster who is *so terrifyingly ugly* that little kids turn to stone *forever* when they see her,' I said. 'And then there are trolls. Trolls used to just live in Norway, but not any more. Now lots of trolls have moved here and trolls stuff little kids inside giant pitta breads and eat them with herrings and salad *three times* a day.'

Magnus was staring at me, silently, but I was just hitting my stride.

'Then, there are werewolves,' I said. 'Watch out for werewolves. They're normal humans most of the time – your teacher or the postman – but at full moon they change. They grow into big hairy monsters, like giant wild wolf men. *They* eat kids too, *especially* little boys. And it's a full moon *very* soon so watch out.'

Magnus's bottom lip was trembling now, although he was still silent, still staring. Did I care? No. I was *so* fed up.

Then I had a thought.

'And you know what?' I said. 'That painting downstairs, of that sea monster? It was probably painted from *life*. It's probably a painting of a sea monster that lives around here. So keep your eyes open. Small boys are the very *first choice* of dinner for a sea monster!'

You know how you say something and you instantly regret it?

I did then.

Magnus was quaking and quivering. He was too scared even to call for Dad. One fat little tear rolled down each of his small chubby cheeks.

I felt bad. I felt grumpy and ashamed. I knew I had gone too far. 'Just joking,' I said. 'There *are* no monsters.'

I stomped over to the window to draw the curtains and shut out the big bright moon.

I gaped. There it was, out there in the bay, just by the island. *Again.* Something *huge* was leaping out of the water.

And this time, I saw it more clearly. It had a long neck, a snout and some weird frilly thing, flapping all around its head.

I couldn't help it.

I shrieked.

I shrieked and I shrieked and I shrieked.

Chapter Four
Shocks in Store

Dad came running in. He saw me, shrieking at the window about something being out there. Something bigger than a whale, with a long neck, a sharp snout, a frilly thing round its head . . .

He saw Magnus, quivering and quaking, whimpering about how I was scaring him by talking about monsters.

Then, with a glare in my direction, Dad whisked Magnus away.

I could hear the two of them talking. Magnus, tucked up in Captain's Cabin, telling Dad all the things I had said. Dad telling Magnus that Fairy Fenella was right and that all the monsters were gone.

Dad stuck his head round the door once Magnus was asleep, and Dad was *not* happy. 'Stan,' he said. 'NO MORE TALK about monsters.'

Then, he stomped off downstairs.

Well, I was not happy either. What a *horrible* coincidence. Me scaring Magnus about monsters and then seeing the big whale thing leaping out there. The big whale thing that looked, well, a bit like the painting: the one in the sitting room, the painting of a sea monster.

No. No, no, no.

The whale thing was *not* a sea monster. Whatever it was, it was definitely *not* a sea monster. Of course it wasn't. Monsters weren't real, any more than fairies were.

All the same, I lay awake. So . . . what sort of whale *was* it then? What kind of whale had a huge long neck and a big snout and something frilly all round its head?

There was not one single whale like that as far as I knew. Whales didn't have long necks: none of them.

I had a thought. Maybe it was a new species. Maybe I had just made an astonishing discovery. Maybe it could be named after its discoverer. Me, Stanley Gubbins. The Gubbins whale.

Then, I had another thought. *Was* it even a whale or was it something else? Perhaps it was some kind of crossbreed: a mix, like some dogs are. Like dalmadoodles are part dalmation and part poodle, or like chugs are part chihuahua and part pug. Or like Bagel, who is a mix of . . . well, Rory isn't quite sure what. Whatever mix makes a dog with short legs, a long body, floppy ears and a curly golden coat.

Was that it? Was this a crossbreed? A mix of . . . what? Eel and whale? Part fish, part mammal, maybe even part lizard too? Because there's a lizard that has a frilly thing round its head, a big flapping frill that it spreads right out when it senses danger.

So . . . could it be part fish, part mammal and part reptile? Was that possible? Maybe it was even a *mutant*, a giant mutant. It could be. It could be some kind of freaky creature, caused by all the muck us humans keep dumping in the sea.

I just did *not* know. All I knew was this. Whatever it was, it was a *big* shock, seeing something that huge, that weird, leaping out of the water.

And next morning – more shocks were in store.

★ ★ ★

Next morning, Dad arranged for Magnus to do a morning's fairy taming with Claudia, then he set off across the beach with me. We were heading for an arrow-shaped signpost at the bottom of the cliff path, with writing on it which read:

TO LIGHTSANDS BAY

The cliff path was steep and rocky. It wound higher and higher and higher, round the side of our cove and up to the headland. I stared as we climbed. I stared left, right and far out to sea, but there was no sign of the whale thing. I couldn't see it anywhere. Shame. I wanted Dad to see it, to find out what he thought it was.

We puffed our way up to the top, then stopped. We looked all around us: at the big views, at Shiversands Cove behind us and at the island far below. It was a dark and craggy island with just one small building huddled on the rocks.

'Tide Island,' said Dad, pointing. 'We can walk to it across the sand at low tide.' Well, we couldn't walk to it now. The only way out to it was over the rickety bridge, stretching from the edge of our cove. Apart from that, it was surrounded by water, completely cut off.

'Tides are very big around here,' said Dad. 'That end of Tide Island, the end nearest our cove, it'll all be sand at low tide.'

I know about tides. It's the moon that makes them happen. Twice every day, the moon slowly pushes the sea right up the beach and then slowly pushes it back down again. Right now, the moon had pushed the tide almost as high as it could go.

We walked on along the headland, and then, ahead of us, far below, there was Lightsands Bay. It was a much bigger bay than our cove with a long sandy beach, wide and curving, with a hilly sort of seaside town stretching up behind it.

There were steep winding streets, all cobbled and narrow, with houses squashed either side, painted pale seaside colours.

A promenade stretched above the beach, the whole way along it. On the promenade there was a lady dressed as a lobster, I have no idea why.

The lobster lady was handing out leaflets. 'Join in the fun and festivities!' she said, pincers wobbling. Then, she gave Dad a leaflet.

LIGHTSANDS BAY FESTIVAL!
A WEEKEND OF FUN AND THRILLS!

FRIDAY NIGHT FIREWORKS!
SATURDAY PARADE!
SUNDAY BEACH BBQ!

FOOD!
TOYS!
CRAFTS!
BEACH GAMES!
FUNFAIR!
FANCY DRESS!
FACE PAINTING!
AND MUCH, MUCH MORE!

Now, the lobster lady was peering closely at Dad, pincers wobbling even more.

Oh no. I knew what was about to happen.

It did.

'Mr Wizzywoz!' she gasped.

Mr Wizzywoz is my dad. He's a kiddie entertainer, with his own show on tv and a *lot* of fans among the under-fives. He spends his time dancing about dressed in baggy green trousers, with a big red nose and a wizardy sort of hat. He goes on wizardy adventures, sings wizardy songs, does magic tricks, acrobatics, unicycling, juggling, balloon animals . . . You name it, Dad does it.

When I was small, I liked Dad being Mr Wizzywoz but *not* now. I keep nagging Dad to get a normal job and be like other mums and dads: to get a grown-up job like a teacher or a doctor. But he never does.

Mum's just as bad. She does acting as her job and she was acting this week. She was being filmed for TV, running about in a big green costume pretending she was an alien and attacking other actors who were pretending they were time travellers.

Dad and the lobster lady got chatting and I had a horrible feeling I knew what would happen next.

It did.

The lobster lady asked Dad to do a turn as Mr Wizzywoz at the Lightsands Bay Festival, down on the beach, on Saturday. I felt my heart sink. Why did I have to have Mr Wizzywoz for a dad? It was just *embarrassing*. Still, at least no one here knew me.

That was when I saw a figure in the distance, standing on the promenade with a pair of binoculars, staring out to sea. I squinted, shocked. No. No, no, *no*! Surely not, how could it be? It could *not* be. Not here, not on my holiday. It *couldn't* be.

But it was. There was no doubt. It was Pearl. Pearl Pankhurst.

Why oh why oh why? Why, of all the kids I knew in town, out of every single one, why did it have to be Pearl Pankhurst here? I ducked, panicking. I did *not* want to see Pearl Pankhurst, not at all.

★ ★ ★

Pearl Pankhurst was the girl who moved into Rory's house. I hung around the day Rory left, waiting to see who the new people were. I was hoping there'd be another boy, one who could help me put the final touches to the trap I was building with Rory.

There *wasn't* another boy. There was Pearl, with her mum.

I could see straight away that Pearl would be no use at all as a trap builder. She was spindly-looking and dainty, and wearing a spotty dress with pink trainers. She was definitely *not* a trap builder.

So I finished the trap on my own. It was a panther trap, because there was a headline in the local paper, which said:

PANTHER ESCAPES FROM ZOO REWARD OFFERED

The reward was for spotting the panther, so the zoo could capture it but I had a better idea, one I told Rory. That, if there was a reward for spotting the panther, there might be a *bigger* reward for actually catching the panther. That maybe the panther was lurking in the woods behind our houses.

We spent three whole days building our trap. Then, I finished it off. Only it was Pearl, not the panther who fell into it.

I was in the Den, under a big willow tree by the river, when I heard a screech. I went running out, in case it was a panther screech.

It wasn't. It was Pearl. She yelled, right in my face, that I was an idiot building a trap right on the path, where someone could fall into it. So I yelled back. I yelled at her that *she* was the idiot for yelling at me, when she should be apologising for ruining my panther trap.

Then, two days later, I found her sitting in the Den, so I told her to get out, as the Den was private, Rory's and mine. She said no. She said under a willow tree was a public space and she had just as much right to sit in the Den as I did.

So I went home and got my water cannon and I ambushed her as she came out of the Den. She yelled at me again. She yelled that I was even more of an idiot than she first thought . . . and how was that possible?

We haven't spoken since. We just glare at each other.

And here she was now, right in front of me, two hundred and fifty miles away from home.

This holiday was turning into a *nightmare*. Then, it got worse.

Chapter Five

The Coastal Clipper

Lightsands Bay had a harbour at the far end. It was small and sheltered, tucked away behind a big stone wall, and full of boats. There were sailing boats, motor boats, big pleasure boats . . .

And, bobbing about at the end of a jetty, an old-style fishing boat. It was a trawler, the kind that drag big nets behind them, scooping up fish as they go. Only this one was painted bright colours and it had a big sign next to it that said:

COASTAL CLIPPER!
LIGHTSANDS BAY BOAT TRIPS!
EVERY TWO HOURS!

A boat trip! Maybe I could get a closer look at the whale thing and show it to Dad, to see what he thought it was.

'Dad, can we do a boat trip?' I said.

Then, I noticed someone sitting in the chair next to the sign. He was a grown man but dressed as a pirate. He was wearing a big pirate hat and a patch over one eye. He had a fake parrot wobbling on one shoulder and he was brandishing a big plastic cutlass.

Oh no. First the lobster lady, now this.

'Dad,' I said. 'I've changed my . . .'

Too late. Dad was walking up to the pirate, wallet out. The pirate leapt up and twirled his big fake moustache. 'I be Pirate Pete, arrrrrr,' he said.

I felt my teeth grind. Did he *have* to talk like that? And worse, look at me – *me* – as if a boy my age would *enjoy* watching a grown-up pretending to be a pirate?

The pirate swept off his hat and gave a low bow. 'Welcome aboard, me hearties,' he said, waving a hand at the boat. Dad was just as bad. He hopped on to the boat, talking to the pirate in *his* pirate voice. Going, 'aharrrrr, me hearty, aharrrr . . .'

I slunk on to the boat behind Dad and slumped down on the long bench seat that stretched all round the sides. It was so unfair. I could have had any dad in the world, but I ended up with this one.

Other tourists started straggling over, all getting the pirate treatment. Once twelve of us were on board, all squashed up on the seats, off the Coastal Clipper chugged. Slowly, it chugged out of the harbour, round a big stone wall sticking right out to sea and then off towards Tide Island.

It was choppier outside the shelter of Lightsands Bay. The boat started bouncing about and the water looked darker: colder and deeper with little frothing white bits on some of the waves.

And Dad got recognised. *Again.* This time by a granny who was sitting right next to me. She sat there – grey hair, grey cardigan, squashy granny shoes – glinting at Dad sideways through her specs. Then, she leaned right over me and tapped Dad on his shoulder.

'Excuse me,' she said, looking thrilled, 'are you Mr Wizzywoz?'

It turned out there were a *lot* of grannies and grandpas on board, who all watched Dad on TV with their grandkids. So Dad sat there, signing things, answering questions and singing bits of Mr Wizzywoz songs.

Then, he turned his attention to the baby.

There was only one baby on board, sitting opposite us, with its mum and its dad. It was a glum-looking thing, with a bald head and a fat face. It was sitting on the dad's lap, stuffed into a stripy onesie, and staring around – toes pointed – all solemn and still.

Dad tried to make the glum baby laugh. He pulled a Ping-Pong ball out of its ear. He sang it a sea shanty. He did a little jig.

Nothing. Not a flicker. The glum baby just stared at him.

Good on that baby!

I tried to ignore it all: Dad, the magic tricks and the sea shanties. Besides, I was busy. I was keeping a watch on the sea, clutching the binoculars, staring left, staring right, looking out for the whale thing.

Slowly, slowly, the boat chugged its way right around Tide Island and into a small creek, right opposite Shiversands Cove. The pirate tied the boat to a big metal ring. Then, we all hopped off the boat and on to a small jetty, all sheltered here from the open sea by the island itself.

'Be back in one hour, me hearties,' said the pirate. 'This landing place — it be no place for boats at low tide, arrrrrrr.'

I felt my teeth grind more. Why not just say 'this creek will be all sand when the tide goes out so the boat will get stuck'? *Much* better.

There was a little machine with tide timetables in it, and a label that said:

WELCOME TO TIDE ISLAND!
TIDE TIMETABLES. PLEASE TAKE ONE!

So I pressed the button and out popped a small booklet. It showed the times of high and low tides for every single day of this year and it also had little pictures showing what kind of moon there was.

'Full moon on Friday,' I said to Dad, which was a *big* mistake. Straight away, Dad threw his head back, then howled, right in my face. I glared at him. And as for the glum baby, did seeing Dad, a fully-grown man, doing a werewolf impression make it move a muscle?

No. It just sat there, squashed into a pack on its dad's back — toes still pointing — and stared.

★ ★ ★

Tide Island was a gloomy sort of place. The far end jutted right out to sea, battered by winds from across the ocean. There were lots of jagged black rocks, and a few bits of grassy stuff struggling to grow. The only building on the island was small and strange, shaped like a tiny lighthouse. It had an arched wooden doorway and a sign outside it, which read:

MILDRED MARCHWOLD WROTE HERE

There was lots more writing underneath the sign. I skimmed through it. It was all stuff about how the building belonged to some olden days writer who lived in our cottage, but came here to do her writing.

Now she was dead and, for some reason, grown-ups had decided to leave the room just as she had it, for visitors to see. I had no idea why they decided that. When we pushed the door open and went inside it was almost empty. No wonder she got her writing done. There was nothing else to do in here. There was no TV, nothing interesting. There was just a chair, a desk, and an olden days machine with a stack of paper next to it.

The machine was huge and heavy-looking and all black, with lots of metal prongs with letters on them. A typewriter, Dad called it. He said it was the way olden days grown-ups used to write books, before laptops. Well, whatever it was, it was heavy. I know because I had a go at lifting it, and I had to heave, really heave.

There was other stuff in there, too: more about Mildred Marchworld. There were things like book covers and notes she wrote but I wasn't much interested. Books aren't really my thing, particularly not ones with fairies and elves on the cover. I did like the window, though. It was a porthole one and it looked straight out to sea.

I stared out but no, there was still no sign of the whale thing. Maybe we'd see it on the way back.

And we did. Well . . . *I* did.

★ ★ ★

I kept scanning on the way back, using the binoculars and scanning left, scanning right, as we chugged out of the creek and away from Shiversands Cove.

It was out there. I *knew* it was out there somewhere and I really, *really* wanted Dad to see it.

Then, I spotted it. We were chugging around Tide Island, turning back towards Lightsands Bay and there it was. It was out at sea, swimming slowly through the water. Clear as clear.

I gaped. It was *huge*. That long neck, that big snouty head, frills flapping around it, that long, *long* body . . .

Dad *had* to see it.

'Dad,' I said, thrusting the binoculars into his hands. 'Look! Quick! Out there. That's what I saw yesterday. That whale thing. What *is* it?'

Dad grabbed the binoculars and looked through them. I waited, expecting him to gasp or say something. To tell me what it was.

He didn't.

He started scanning around, scanning left, scanning right. What was Dad doing? Why wasn't he looking at the whale thing, the mutant, whatever it was?

'Look!' I said, guiding him, pointing the binoculars straight at it. 'Right there. *There*!'

Dad was still peering and shaking his head. 'Nope,' he said. 'Can't see it.'

But . . . it was *there*. Slap bang in front of his eyes. How could Dad *not* see it?

The whale thing turned and stared straight at us. It gave a big swish of its tail and slapped it down on the water. Which startled me, so I yelped.

And now it was Dad who was staring. He was turning and staring at *me*. Me! Narrowing his eyes, as if he was baffled by the yelping, as if he was wondering what I was up to.

That was when I knew. That was when I realised.

Dad couldn't see it. The whale thing, the whatever, even though it was clear as clear, Dad could *not* see it.

I looked all around the boat and I realised something else. It wasn't just Dad. It was *all* the grown-ups. Not one grown-up could see the whale thing. They were all staring straight through it, not seeing it at all. They were looking out to sea, as if that enormous whale thing simply wasn't there.

Which was when I heard a chuckle: the chuckle of a baby.

I turned. The baby, not glum any more, was waving its fat little arms and trying to clap its fat little hands. Its eyes were popping with excitement.

That *enormous* creature swimming out there, there were only two people on this boat who could see it.

The baby.

And me.

Chapter Six
Magic Eyes

Back at Shiversands Cottage, I huddled in the sitting room, struggling to think, struggling to come up with a reason, some kind of explanation. Why – *how* – was it possible that I could see that enormous creature out there in the sea, and Dad couldn't?

It *wasn't* possible. It just wasn't.

I tried and tried but I could *not* come up with one good reason, not one explanation for how that was possible. Only this one . . .

That the thing out there, the big greeny-grey thing cruising around just outside our cove, was a monster. It had to be. It was an actual, real-life sea monster, some kind of magical creature. And the reason I could see it but Dad couldn't, was this: because I had magic eyes and Dad didn't.

No. It was *not* possible. I did *not* have magic eyes. There was no such thing as magic eyes. But magic eyes were the only explanation. There was no other explanation that made sense, none at all.

I thought back, back to the journey to Shiversands Cove, with Magnus in his car seat going on and on, telling me all the things Fairy Fenella said about magic eyes. How little kids are born with them, born with magic eyes. Special eyes. How some little kids, the lucky ones, see some kind of magical creature and keep hold of their magic eyes forever and ever.

But, even supposing Fairy Fenella *was* right about magic eyes, I was *not* one of those kids. I definitely wasn't. I never saw any magical creatures as a little kid, nothing that would help me keep hold of my magic eyes: no fairies, or elves, or goblins, no dragons, no monsters. Nothing.

Although . . .

I stopped and thought.

I thought right back, to something that happened when I was four years old, a dream I had. At least, I *thought* it was a dream.

I was in Norway, visiting my Norwegian granny, up in the mountains. It was late, and I was supposed to be tucked up in bed, fast asleep but days are long and light in Norway in summer, and I couldn't sleep, not at all. So I knelt on my bed and stared out of the window, up at the mountain.

And that's where I saw it.

It was a monster, crouched on a ledge, high up on the mountain. The monster was far away but I could see it was huge. It was as tall as a giraffe and scaly like a dragon, with short arms, long claws and two giant wings which it started flapping.

Then, the monster took off. It soared down the mountain, huge wings flapping, flying closer and closer to Granny's house and to me, staring out of the window.

The monster saw me. It flew towards my window, and hovered outside.

I stared out at the monster and the monster stared in at me. It had shiny yellow eyes, a long flicking red tongue and big blobs of dribble trickling out of its snout. I knew it was much too big to get in through the window but I could hear it hissing and I started screaming. I screamed for Mum, I screamed for Dad, and they came running in, just as the monster flew off.

Mum and Dad both sat with me after that. They sat and held my hands, as I gibbered and whimpered, and told them what I just saw.

Dad said I was dreaming. He told me again and again that it was all a dream. Mum told me the same thing had happened to her. That she had a dream like that once, when she was as small as me, and, just like me, she was convinced her dream was real, when it wasn't.

But suppose Mum and Dad were wrong, suppose I *wasn't* dreaming? Suppose it was true, was real, and I really *did* see that monster? Then *that* would be why I kept my magic eyes and why I could see *this* monster now.

So, I huddled there in the sitting room, head spinning. What now? What should I do? Did I need to do anything?

Maybe not.

That monster was far out at sea, a long way off. It was nowhere near our cove and there was no reason to think it would attack. After all, it showed no sign of attacking the boat and something that big could have charged at the boat and caused a *lot* of damage.

But it didn't.

Besides, I have read hundreds of monster stories and one thing I know. Not all monsters are bad. There are good monsters too, friendly, helpful monsters, and this could be one of them.

So, although I would *prefer* to have a holiday without glimpses of a far away sea monster, as long as far away was where it stayed, I could cope. In fact, I could even do some drawings of it and send them to Rory. I could tell him all about it, tell him what he was missing.

And anyway, whales swim thousands of miles each year, so sea monsters probably did too. This sea monster was probably just passing through. It would leave soon; maybe it was gone already.

Just then, I heard Dad's feet clumping into the house. He stuck his head round the sitting room door. 'Stan,' he said. 'I have a little favour to ask you.'

★ ★ ★

'No,' I said. 'No, no, NO! I will NOT do it.' Then, I shook my head, and folded my arms.

Because Dad wanted me to be Wicked Wanda.

Wicked Wanda is a witch who keeps interfering with Mr Wizzywoz's plans. Wicked Wanda is also Mum but Mum wasn't here.

'I need a stand-in,' said Dad. 'So I can practise a new routine for the Lightsands Bay Festival.'

56

Then he threw himself to his knees and clasped his hands. 'Please, please,' he said staring up at me and clutching my leg. 'I'm begging you.'

'Get up,' I said, pushing him off. 'There's no way am I doing it. I do *not* feel like being Wicked Wanda and there is not one *single thing* in the whole world that you can say to make me change my mind.'

There – that told him.

But then Dad got this crafty look on his face. 'If you stand in as Wicked Wanda,' he said, 'I'll teach you how to use the lasso.'

Oh, that was *unfair*.

I have been *begging* Dad to teach me how to use his lasso. It's a real one, like cowboys use. Dad uses it as part of his Mr Wizzywoz routine and every time I beg him, he says he's too busy, or it's too precious, or we need a bigger space than our back garden. He has hundreds of reasons, all adding up to the same answer.

No.

Up until today.

Which is how I ended up prancing around the beach, standing in as Wicked Wanda.

★ ★ ★

I'll spare you the details. It was a terrible story: some race to find buried treasure. Maybe little kids would find it thrilling, but I didn't.

So I had to prance about, cackling, with a hunting horn I had to keep blowing. And Dad kept lassoing me, again and again, until he got the routine just right.

Then, at *last*, it was over, and I got to use the lasso. Dad stuck a picnic chair on the beach. He showed me how to do it, and I practised. I practised and practised, concentrating really hard.

Time whizzed by as I stood there, lassoing the picnic chair, getting better and better. It turned out I was a natural and I was enjoying myself so much, and concentrating so hard, that I almost forgot about the sea monster.

Then, I looked up . . . and there it was. Only it wasn't out at sea. No. Not any more. Now it was right here, here in Shiversands Cove.

I felt my legs go wobbly. The monster poked its head out of the water and swivelled it around. I knew what that monster was doing: spyhopping. That's what whales do; they poke their heads up and look around.

I backed away.

But why? *Why* was the monster spyhopping? What was it looking around for? And why was it here, in Shiversands Cove? Why was it so *close*?

I backed further away, further up the beach. I could hear Magnus just behind me, sitting on the sand, chatting to his fairy. By now, my legs were so wobbly that they wouldn't hold me up any more and I collapsed on the sand.

Magnus let out a huge shriek. 'DON'T SIT ON HARRY!' he shouted.

Which was when I felt small, sharp teeth nip my behind, as, out from underneath me, something zoomed. Something which was wearing sparkly gold shorts. Something which was flapping sparkly gold wings. Something which was chattering furiously and gnashing two very big front teeth, more like fangs, right in my face.

A fairy. It was a small, angry fairy.

Chapter Seven

Harry the Horrible

It was like being in the middle of a dream: the weirdest dream of my whole life. This could *not* be happening.

First, there was a sea monster in the bay and now there was a fairy in the garden. And there was no way of talking to Dad about it because, well, what could I say?

'Dad, there is a sea monster in our cove. Oh, and Harry the fairy is also real. But you can't see either of them because you don't have magic eyes.'

No. I couldn't say that. How could I? There are some things you just *can't* say to a dad.

To make matters worse, Harry the fairy was *horrible*.

He had sparkly fairy shorts and sparkly fairy wings but he also had weird eyes: mean little eyes,

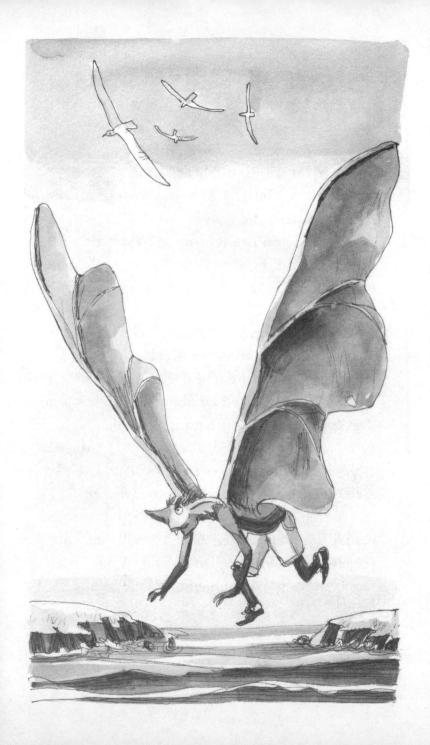

angry eyes, which were a dark reddish colour. He had bushy eyebrows, creepy curved fingernails and low-set ears. His ears were as weird as his eyes. They were long and narrow, and a tiny bit furry, laid flat on his little fairy head.

And Harry the Horrible did *not* like me, not since I almost sat on him.

He glared at me and chattered his teeth. Then, he started sniffing round my head, sniffing my hair, sniffing in my ears, sniffing wherever he could.

He was behaving like Bagel. That's what Bagel always did, every walk we went on; every time Bagel met another dog, he'd start sniffing it.

Now, Harry started sniffing right in my face. 'Get OFF me,' I yelled, batting him off. 'Pest!'

'Don't be a *horrid*, Stan,' tutted Magnus, wagging his finger. 'Harry's not a pest. He's a little fairy. And he wants to be your friend.'

'He does NOT want to be my friend,' I said, batting him off again. 'And anyway, he's not a proper fairy. Where's his wand? Aren't fairies supposed to have wands and do little bits of fairy magic?'

Although I was quite glad Harry *didn't* have a wand. He might be even worse. Then Harry swooped down and started sniffing round my knees. 'STOP that!' I yelled, kicking up with my knee. Harry didn't like that. He flew up and flapped his sparkly wings in my face, hissing and gnashing his teeth.

'You know what?' I said. 'I'm not even sure he *is* a fairy. Look at those teeth and the furry ears. He's creepy. More like a flying hobgoblin.'

But I had bigger things to worry about than Harry, like a sea monster, here, in Shiversands Cove.

I left Magnus and Dad in the cove and went back up to the cottage. I had a *lot* of thinking to do. That painting, the one in the sitting room, it was looking likely that it *was* of the monster, so the sea monster was probably *not* passing through. This was probably where the sea monster lived.

I checked the painting. It was old. It had a signature I couldn't read, and a date on it: 1904, a long time ago. Was it a very old sea monster, then? How long did sea monsters live? Hundreds of years? Or was it a *family* of sea monsters? Was this a grandchild of the sea monster in the painting?

I had a scary thought: maybe there was more than one sea monster. Maybe there were lots of sea monsters, a big family, and they all looked alike.

No. If they were family they would do some swimming together, surely. So it was probably just the one monster I had to worry about.

Still, it couldn't be a ferocious monster because if that sea monster *was* ferocious, people would know about it. There would be gruesome discoveries: fishing boats with jagged holes in them and no sign of their owner; tourists disappearing without trace.

No. There could *not* be a ferocious monster in this bit of the sea without people knowing it because, even if they couldn't see it, even if they didn't have magic eyes, they could see its effects. So the monster was probably harmless, like a basking shark.

Yes, that was it. It was big, it was ugly, but it was harmless. It just swam about, not bothering humans. It wasn't interested in feeding on humans, just on fish. It could even be a vegetarian.

Unlike Harry.

★ ★ ★

It turned out that Harry the Horrible liked meat. I was in the kitchen, making myself a ham roll, and then I went to the fridge to get a glass of milk. In Harry swooped, through the kitchen door. He helped himself to my ham and then shot off.

I was annoyed with Harry for stealing, but also astonished. Ham wasn't a very, well, *fairylike* sort of food. Weren't fairies supposed to like sugary things like little pink cupcakes and sugar lumps? That sort of thing?

Not Harry.

Next, I caught him trying to eat Magnus's hamster. I went upstairs and there he was, licking his lips and trying to squeeze himself through the bars of the hamster cage. I yanked him away, hurled him out of the window, and slammed it shut.

'Magnus,' I bellowed down the stairs, 'keep your fairy under control! Put it on a lead or something. It just tried to eat the hamster!'

'Stan,' said a cross voice behind me.

Dad was standing there, frowning. 'Don't be mean. Let Magnus enjoy his fairy game.'

I stomped off to look in the rock pools. I was fed up with Harry the Horrible and still fretting about having a sea monster, even a harmless one, in our cove. As I was clambering about on the rocks, I heard two noises: first, chattering noises and then the sound of small fluttering wings.

I looked up and there was Harry, zooming across the beach, chattering. Zooming towards me.

Oh no! Not again. He didn't *like* me so why did he have to keep bothering me, sniffing around me? I filled a bucket with water. I was ready. One sniff of me and Harry was getting a drenching: time to see if *this* fairy had waterproof wings.

Then, I heard another noise: a much bigger one, a loud slapping noise. I went cold. That noise, it was an angry noise, a warning noise. And it was also in the cove.

I turned and stared.

There it was, the sea monster. It was right there, in the middle of the cove. It was looking straight at me and slapping its huge great tailfin on the surface of the water, smacking it up and down, up and down, so that water sprayed everywhere.

Then, the frilly thing all around its head shot out sideways and stood out, all stiff around its head. I knew what that frill was. It was a threat.

Then, the sea monster started to swim fast, straight towards me.

So I ran. I scrambled round the rocks and back up the beach. Who knew how far a sea monster could rear or how far it could grab?

I ran back to the cottage, straight into the sitting room and threw myself down, on the sofa. I sat there, panicking because, all of a sudden, that sea monster did *not* look harmless. Not harmless at all.

And I remembered something. Morris. Morris the dolphin.

Morris had been on the news a few weeks ago. He was a dolphin that had been swimming with tourists for years and years, playing with them in the bay and letting them tickle him and bounce balls off his nose, everything.

Then, one day, Morris turned. He attacked a tourist, viciously. He dragged them round the bay and tried to drown them. And later, he did it again.

That was it.

Morris was no longer safe to be around tourists. Morris was a danger. Morris had gone rogue, the news reporter said.

Was that what was happening here in Shiversands Cove? Had a harmless sea monster, one which had been swimming here for years and years, now gone rogue?

Chapter Eight
Sunset Swim

I sat, quaking, in the sitting room. Then, I noticed
a big box with a big label on the front, which read:

**SHIVERSANDS COTTAGE
VISITOR INFORMATION**

The box had leaflets inside, lots of leaflets, so I
started sorting through them. They all showed
things to do around here – things that did *not*
involve the sea. I made a big pile. We could hire
bikes, go on forest trails, visit a working farm,
a woollen mill, a chocolate factory, make some
pottery, all sorts.

Yes. That's what I could do. Turn this into an
activity holiday. I could keep us busy one day at
a time – and nowhere near the sea. I grabbed a

leaflet and went to see Dad. 'Dad,' I said, waving the leaflet in his face, 'can we go here tomorrow? And take a picnic?'

★ ★ ★

Next morning I sat, watching out of the car window, as we drove further and further away from the sea, further and further inland. Then, there it was. Up on a tall hill, towering over the town was a castle, Cleeston Hill Castle.

Cleeston Hill Castle was big and square, with lots of battlements. Some of it was ruins, some of it not.

'Claudia might be here already,' said Magnus, jiggling in his car seat. 'Claudia *and* her cousin!'

The castle plan had got bigger over night. Now, Claudia was coming too and Claudia's cousin, who was staying somewhere in Lightsands Bay, and their mums and dads.

'A cousin,' said Magnus, clasping his hands. 'Claudia has a *cousin*! And I am going to meet the cousin! Today! At the castle!'

Magnus was jiggling with excitement. Magnus loves cousins. We have five: two toddlers, who wreck things; two four-year-olds, who hunt fairies; and Ned, who is my age. Ned is the *only* good thing about having cousins.

I just hoped Claudia had a Ned for a cousin.

We parked near the castle, got tickets and then walked through a big stone archway on to a wide green lawn with the castle battlements stretching right around it. There were a group of people in the middle of the lawn, stretching out a picnic rug.

'There she is!' shrieked Magnus, waving and hurtling towards them. 'There's Claudia!'

I could see Claudia too. I could see some grown-ups and . . .

Oh no.

I stopped and gaped. That girl standing there, she must be Claudia's cousin. She was also Pearl, Pearl Pankhurst.

★ ★ ★

Pearl's grown-ups started shrieking at Dad and Dad started shrieking back, all about being new neighbours back home and now meeting here, about what an astonishing coincidence it was, and about how they could *not* believe it.

Well, nor could I. It just wasn't *fair*.

Dad was beaming at me. 'Someone your own age at last,' he said, as if being the same age as Pearl made us friends. Which it didn't.

Then, Dad waved his hand. 'Explore,' he said. 'Have fun!'

Fun? Where was the fun in being stuck here with Pearl? I stomped off.

Pearl stomped after me. 'I'm not happy to see you either,' she said, scowling. 'But if we're going exploring let's call a truce and start again.'

I turned and gaped. 'A truce? Going exploring?' I said. 'There is no truce and *we* are not going exploring . . . *I* am.'

I hadn't finished. 'For your information,' I said, 'a good neighbour, such as my friend Rory, has a sense of humour. If *Rory* had fallen into my trap he would have found it funny.'

Now, Pearl had her hands on her hips. 'Well,' she said, 'for *your* information, a good neighbour, like my friend Ruby who lived four doors down from me, would NOT make traps in stupid places like on the path.'

'Course she wouldn't,' I said. 'Girls don't build traps.'

For some reason, me saying that made Pearl's jaw drop and her eyes narrow. 'Is that so?' she said. Then she leaned right in my face. 'For your *further* information,' she hissed, 'your trap was NOT a good trap. Your trap was a *beginner* trap. I could have done that trap way better.'

Now I could feel *my* jaw drop. The cheek of it! Pearl telling me, an expert trap builder, that my trap was a beginner trap.

She hadn't finished. She jabbed a finger at me. 'And another thing,' she said. 'Your den – it could be twice as good as it is. And disguised. IF you built it where *I* would build a den.'

I glared at her, as hard as I could.

'And STOP glaring,' she snapped. 'It makes you look like a gorilla.'

A gorilla?

Now, I like gorillas. In fact, they're probably my second favourite after whales. But I did *not* look like a gorilla.

So I stomped off to go exploring on my own and Pearl stomped off and started running around, exploring with Magnus and Claudia and helping them look for castle fairies.

I was miserable, all day long: fed up; lonely; missing Rory; hating this holiday and most of all, worrying about the sea monster. Even if today was OK, what about all the other days?

But today *wasn't* OK because later that afternoon, the grown-ups decided on one final plan for the day. Back to Lightsands Bay for a swim.

★ ★ ★

The sun was low in the sky when we got to Lightsands Bay and the water looked dark. Very dark. 'Dad,' I said. 'I want to dig.' I got out the spade because I knew one thing; I was *not* swimming.

Magnus was swimming though and Dad and everyone else: everyone except Pearl. 'Mum,' she said, 'I want to read back at our apartment, out on the balcony.'

Pearl and her grown-ups had an apartment in a big building right on the promenade so Pearl got the keys and marched off, nose in the air as she walked past me. A minute later she appeared out on a second-floor balcony, looking straight over the beach. She had a book in her hand and she waved down at her mum.

Then Magnus and Claudia started waving too, but not at Pearl: at the cliff top. They were jumping up and down, clapping their hands, waving and pointing. I turned. Oh no. There was Harry, a tiny shape with sparkly golden wings zooming over the cliff top from Shiversands Cove. Zooming towards Lightsands Bay.

'Harry!' shouted Magnus, jumping up and down and waving. 'Harry! Cooee! We're over here!'

'We're going swimming, Harry,' bellowed Claudia. 'You come too!'

All the grown-ups started making gooey faces, the sort grown-ups make when little kids do things they find enchanting, like pretending to have a fairy friend.

Then, Claudia wagged her finger at me. 'Stan, don't be horrid to Harry today,' she said.

She turned to the grown-ups. 'Stan doesn't like our fairy,' she told them. 'Stan shouts at him.' And all the grown-ups looked at me: no gooey faces any more, just frowns.

★ ★ ★

I could *not* concentrate on my digging. My eyes kept straying down to the sea, scanning the horizon. Jittering. Staring at Magnus, splashing about, holding on to his bodyboard, kicking his legs, while Dad pulled him through the water. Staring out over the water.

Here came Harry. He was zooming straight towards me, little nostrils flaring, sniffing all around my head. But I was ready for him. I had leftovers from the picnic in my hand: a big chunk of pepperoni. I wafted it right in front of his small sniffing nose.

Harry licked his lips and went to grab it but I was too quick. I ran off with it. I hurtled down the beach and then chucked the pepperoni out to sea, as far and as high as I could.

Off Harry went, swooping out over the water towards the pepperoni chunk. Then, just as he snapped it up, I spotted something. Something that was swimming round the end of Tide Island, swimming straight towards Lightsands Bay, swerving fast through the water. Swerving towards Dad and Magnus.

I got a cold, cold feeling. Dad and Magnus were right in its path, backs to the sea monster, splashing through the water

I ran. I hurled myself as fast as I could through the water, out towards Dad, towards Magnus. I grabbed hold of Magnus, dragged him off his bodyboard and back towards the beach. Then I tumbled him on to the sand.

'GET OUT OF THE WATER!' I shrieked at Dad. 'The sea monster . . . it's heading this way!'

Chapter Nine

In the Shed

A silly thoughtless prank, that's what Dad yelled at me, among other things. As for Magnus, he stood on the beach, dripping and wagging his finger right in my face, telling me that scaring a little boy of four enjoying a splashabout was *actual* bullying.

Dad marched me home and I skulked off to the shed. I sat in there, panicking. My plan of finding things to do on land each day, it would *never* work. Of course it wouldn't. *Never.*

Magnus loves swimming. Magnus averages about three swims a day. I might stay on the beach but Magnus wouldn't and nor would Dad. And we had another eight days here. Eight days, with Magnus having three swims a day, was *twenty-four* chances for a sea monster to attack. Which it would, I was sure it would. And this time, it might succeed.

I panicked all evening and most of the night. What could I do? One boy against a sea monster, a sea monster five times my size. *At least.*

And all on my own . . .

Except I *wasn't* all on my own because next morning, as I sat on the patio staring out to sea, some walkers arrived. Three walkers were coming over the cliff top. It was Pearl's mum, Pearl's dad and Pearl. They were walking down the path, towards the beach.

I expected Pearl to ignore me: to stick her nose in the air, stomp right past, and on to Claudia's house. But she didn't.

She said something to her mum, then came scrambling up the rocks, through the gate, and up our garden. She sat down next to me, pale and trembling.

'I saw it too,' she said.

★ ★ ★

Weather changes fast by the sea. Big grey clouds started whooshing across the sky, the sun disappeared, then rain started falling.

I ran for the shed, Pearl right behind me, and we huddled inside, rain drumming down hard on the window. 'Every monster story I have *ever* read,' I said, teeth clacking, 'every single one – it's all about the kids being smarter than the monster is, and outwitting it in some way. So that's all we have to do: come up with a plan to outwit it.'

'And there's two of us,' said Pearl, teeth also clacking. 'It's two kids' brains against one monster brain so we'll be a *lot* smarter than it is. We'll come up with an outwitting plan easily. Probably before dinnertime.'

We didn't.

We sat. We thought. We panicked.

'The sea monster,' I said, trying to think positive, 'it doesn't seem to have *scary* skills. Nothing sneaky. No tricky magic skills, like turning kids to stone, or teleporting, or breathing fire. Nothing like that.'

'No,' said Pearl, doing her best to nod and look confident. 'Just a straightforward, ordinary sea monster, that's what we're dealing with.'

Then she bit her lip. 'Although,' she said, and now she was gulping, 'it's got very good swimming skills. It's as fast as a speedboat and it is very *big*. And we'll need to keep away from its teeth. They're very sharp and there are *lots* of them.'

'It has good leaping skills, too,' I said, also gulping. 'It's a *huge* leaper. It leaps about the height of this cottage. And that tail, we'll have to watch out for that tailfin. One swish of that could probably knock a kid unconscious.'

We sat there, gulping more. Thinking more. Panicking more. But *still* nothing came. We had no plan, no way to outwit it. *Nothing*.

'Maybe it has a weak spot,' I said. 'Lots of monsters do, in the stories.'

Pearl started nodding, hard. 'That'll be it,' she said, 'a weak spot. We just need to find its weak spot, like story kids do. At least half of the story kids do.'

'More I'd say,' I said, also nodding hard. 'Sixty per cent, maybe even seventy.'

But I wondered.

Did this sea monster have a weak spot? Or was it one of those monsters with no weak spot at all? Then I realised something.

Of *course* it had a weak spot. The sea monster, it could *not* live out of water.

I thought Pearl would be impressed when I told her, but she wasn't. She started biting her lip.

'But how does that help us?' she said. 'Two kids our size, we can't get a sea monster out of the water. How can we? We can't lift it, can't drag it. Nothing.'

Then, she jumped up and stared out of the window. 'It's out there somewhere,' she said, and there was a big wobble in her voice now. 'And there's *nothing* we can do.'

I stared too, out of the window, down the garden, all the way out to Tide Island.

Only Tide Island *wasn't* an island now, not now the tide was low, not now everywhere was sand. Tide Island was on the sand. Sand stretched all the way out of our cove, right over to Tide Island, right over to the creek.

That was when I turned and looked at Pearl. 'Maybe there *is* something we can do,' I said slowly. 'Maybe there *is* a way to get a sea monster out of the water.'

And there was: by using the tide.

★ ★ ★

'So, the plan,' I said, 'let's go over it one more time. High tide tonight, we bait the water in the creek on Tide Island and wait for the sea monster.'

'Then,' said Pearl, nodding, 'when the sea monster arrives you lasso it, using the Mr Wizzywoz lasso.'

'And you keep it distracted,' I said, 'by throwing the netting, the big heavy fishing net, over its head.'

Keeping it distracted was important. Once it was lassoed I had to crouch down and tie the other end of the lasso to the big metal ring, but crouching down would make me *very* close to the sea monster's teeth.

'And while I keep it distracted and struggling,' Pearl said, 'you – quickly and safely – do the tying.'

'Then,' I said, 'all we have to do is go back home and wait for the tide to go out.'

'And that will be it,' Pearl said. 'The sea monster will be stranded. Beached on the sand. Despatched.'

Then we both started nodding.

'It's a good plan: a safe plan,' said Pearl, trying *very* hard to look confident in our plan. 'The sea monster can't get us. Not if we're on Tide Island and it's in the sea.'

I nodded. 'The worst that can happen,' I said, 'is that our plan fails. And then we'll just have to think of another plan.'

But I wondered. Was that really the worst that could happen?

Chapter Ten
The Plan Begins

There was one problem with our plan: a *big* problem. High tide that night was just before seven but the grown-ups had a plan for seven, a plan to watch the fireworks, over in Lightsands Bay.

By six o'clock we were all eating fish and chips on the balcony of Pearl's apartment, right above the seafront of Lightsands Bay. Crowds of people were milling about below us, all over the promenade. Excited kids were running around with painted faces, and there were stalls selling food and drinks. Grown-ups were stuffing down hot dogs, a brass band was playing and there were banners up everywhere.

FRIDAY NIGHT FIREWORKS AND FUN!
STARTS SEVEN O'CLOCK!

OPENING LIGHTSANDS BAY FESTIVAL WITH A BANG!

I sat on the balcony with Pearl, eating fast and feeling nervous. Tonight, for me and for Pearl, there would be no fireworks, no fun here in Lightsands Bay.

No. We *had* to get away. We had a sea monster to trap, back in Shiversands Cove and there was only one way to do it: with a big fat *lie*.

Now, I'm not a big fan of lying to dads and mums. For a start, I usually get found out. But with a sea monster on the loose, there was no choice.

Soon, the grown-ups were ready to go: standing up, chatting about how it was time to go, time to get a good spot on the beach for watching the fireworks.

And *that* was when we swung into action.

Pearl got the lie going first. She stuck her head on one side. 'Mum,' she said. 'Please, *please* can we stay here? Stan and me? We want to watch the fireworks from the balcony, on our own.'

I tugged on Dad's sleeve. 'Can we, Dad?' I said. 'Just us, not with you, not with the little kids. The balcony's got a brilliant view.'

'And we'll be very responsible,' said Pearl, plastering this earnest, sensible look all over her face. 'We won't use the cooker or do anything dangerous.'

The grown-ups did some discussing, on and on and *on*, using long words to each other like independence and responsibility and common sense.

I had my fingers crossed. This had to work.

And it *did* work. *Finally*.

The grown-ups came up with a long list of rules and we stood there, doing lots of nodding, looking as earnest and sensible as we could. In the end, they left us there, alone on the balcony. We watched them trooping on to the promenade, Magnus and Claudia skipping and waving, as they all disappeared down the steps, and on to the beach.

Then, off we shot, out of Pearl's apartment and down the stairs. We dodged through the crowds and headed for the cliff path. Headed back towards Shiversands Cove.

★ ★ ★

Shiversands Cove was dark and silent. There were big shadows all around us. The sun was sinking

low and the sea was stretching away, darker and darker and darker. Out there, Tide Island was a big dark shadow, looming out of the water.

Quaking, we got our equipment and scurried across the bridge, looking left, looking right. Looking for that long neck, that swishing tail, those goggling eyes.

But there was no sign of it.

We could hear faint noises coming from Lightsands Bay, the sounds of music and laughter, but here there was only silence and the sounds of the sea.

We scrambled off the bridge, and on to Tide Island, then headed for the creek. We baited the water and stood there, waiting: me clutching the lasso, Pearl clutching the netting.

I gulped. I couldn't help it. What had seemed like a good plan in daylight did *not* seem such a good plan right now: not here, all on our own. Questions were barging about in my brain. Questions I did *not* want to think about.

Questions like – if a boy is good at lassoing a picnic chair, will he also be good at lassoing a sea monster?

And – how much *harder* is it to lasso a moving sea monster than a non-moving picnic chair?

And – is the height of a sea monster's head a height that a lasso will actually reach?

And – is a bit of old fishing net enough to distract a sea monster while a boy crouches to tie a lasso to a big metal ring?

And – if a sea monster is *not* distracted, what will it do to a crouching boy?

Question after question after question.

But there was one question I *didn't* ask myself. The sea monster, is it the *only* monster around?

★ ★ ★

Still we stood there, quaking more and more.

'Where is it?' said Pearl, teeth clacking. 'Where?'

'Could be anywhere,' I said, knees knocking. 'Out at sea, behind the island, anywhere.'

'This *is* going to work, isn't it?' Pearl said, with a whimper.

'It has to,' I said. Then I gulped. 'And it *will*.'

But where was the sea monster? Where? The sun was almost gone now. Sinking right below the horizon.

Then, I heard fluttering behind me. Oh *no*! Not Harry, not *now*.

But here he was, a small flying nuisance. He was sniffing at me, sniffing all around me, and making little throaty growling noises: strange, agitated noises.

I swiped at him. This was no time for a fairy to start bothering me. I had a sea monster to sort out. I scanned left and right. Where was it? *Where*?

Now Harry was growling in my ear and sniffing at it. Sniffing and sniffing, worse than *ever*. I swiped him away with the back of my hand.

And then, far out at sea, I saw something.

'There,' I said, peering through the darkness. 'Is that it? That big shape? Far away?'

It was hard to tell. There wasn't enough light to be sure. But just then, the moon began to rise. Slowly, slowly, up in the sky.

A huge moon.

A bright moon.

A *full* moon.

And *that* was when I heard howling. Coming from right behind me.

Chapter Eleven
Monster Attack

The howling, what was it?

I turned and gaped.

It was Harry, Harry the fairy. His small fairy head was thrown right back as he howled up at the huge bright moon.

A chill went right through me, right from the top of my head to the ends of my toes. Something was happening to Harry. He was starting to grow, to grow taller, then taller still.

And Harry was growing hairier: much, much hairier. Hairs were sprouting all over him. Thick hairs, dark hairs were growing all over his arms, his legs, his face, even all over his wings. Everywhere.

And still he howled. Howled and howled up at the huge moon.

That huge *full* moon.

'Run,' I said to Pearl, grabbing her hand. 'RUN!'

We ran to the only place I could think of, the only building on Tide Island: Mildred Marchwold's writing room. We wrenched the door open, hurled ourselves inside, slammed the door shut and bolted it. Then we both stared out of the window, shocked and terrified. What was happening? How could Harry the fairy have turned into *that*? That towering shadow, silhouetted against the huge white moon. How?

He now had the snarling face of a . . . what . . . a *wolf*? He had huge hairy legs and huge hairy arms. His huge hairy wings were spread out and flapping.

I cowered and so did Pearl, as Harry – or whatever it was that Harry had become – raised his huge hairy face to the sky and howled.

Howl after howl after howl. Bloodcurdling howls. Spine-tingling howls. Howls that made my knees knock, my hair stand on end. Howls that sent shivers right through me.

'What is it? What is he?' said Pearl, quivering. 'A monster? But what sort? What sort of monster is *that*?'

'I don't know,' I said. 'A mix? Some horrible mix of werewolf and fairy? A . . . a *werefairy*? Is that what he is?'

'But . . . we had plans for a sea monster,' said Pearl, panicking more. 'We had no plans for a werefairy, no plans at all.'

She was clutching my arm now and I clutched back.

What could we do? Stay here and hide? Wait until the full moon was gone and he was Harry again?

No.

That monster, that werefairy, it was part wolf and wolves can smell things miles away. He'd smell us out.

And he did, right then.

His head went up and he sniffed the air. Then he turned and stared. He gave a snarl and up he came, leaping and bounding over the rocks, a huge dark shadow on huge hairy paws.

Pearl shrieked and backed away across the room. So did I. Because now the werefairy was here, staring straight in through the window, vicious red eyes glowing bright as flames. He bared his huge sharp fangs, fangs made for ripping, made for tearing. He sniffed with his huge hairy nose, licked his lips with a slobbering tongue and then, he was gone.

'Where is he?' said Pearl, her voice quivering. 'Where?'

'I don't know,' I said. 'I just don't know.'

But then we found out.

Thud . . . Thud . . . Thud . . .

The werefairy was outside the door.

★ ★ ★

We stood there, listening to the noises, the loud grunting noises, the threatening noises, the hungry noises, coming from outside, as the werefairy put his shoulder to the door.

A *thud* . . . then a pause. A *thud* . . . then a pause.

Something happened then, to me. Something changed, because I knew this: that door was *not* built to keep out a werefairy.

I looked at Pearl and I saw, by the furious light in her eye, that the same thing had happened to her.

'So, we can wait . . .' I said.

Pearl looked at me and nodded. 'Or we can DO something,' she said.

And we did.

It took us seconds to get into position. Pearl stood by the door, hand on the bolt. I stood to one side, up on the chair, the big heavy typewriter clutched in my arms.

We listened to the werefairy outside the door.

A *thud* . . . then a pause. A *thud*. . . then a pause.

A *thud* . . . and Pearl timed it perfectly. She unbolted the door and flung it wide open just as the werefairy's shoulder was thudding against it.

In lurched the werefairy, tottering and caught by surprise, all off balance. I was waiting.

I raised the typewriter as high as I could, then brought it crashing down on his huge werefairy head. I hoped I'd knock him out and make him keel over, make him fall to the ground, unconscious.

I didn't.

The werefairy yowled. He yelped. He staggered. He clutched his head. He roared in pain. But he did *not* keel over.

Still, we ran for it. Back down the cliff path, over the rocks and towards the bridge. But two kids on foot can *not* outrun a flying werefairy. We heard the flap of huge wings behind us and the snarls of a werefairy with a *very* sore head.

Then he landed, blocking our path: a huge hairy werefairy, much taller than Dad, sniffing and snarling and licking his lips.

We cowered up there on the rocks. Water was behind us and below us. The werefairy was ahead. Nothing could save us now.

Nothing.

Chapter Twelve
The Chase

I will never forget what happened next. *Never.*

I cowered on the rocks, Pearl cowering beside me. Then, far out in Shiversands Cove, we heard a splash: the huge splash of a sea monster leaping out of the water.

Across the cove, the sea monster came surging. It surged towards the rocks, towards me, towards Pearl . . . towards the werefairy.

Then, right by the rocks, the sea monster reared up. It towered above us. The huge frill shot out and stood up, all around its head. Its long snout started snapping open and shut, open and shut. Then:

SMACK!

Down went its huge tailfin. Up and down, up and down, smacking flat on the water. Drenching me, drenching Pearl, with huge showers of spray . . . and drenching the werefairy.

Head to foot, that huge hairy werefairy was *soaked*. He was soaked from the top of his huge hairy head to the ends of his huge hairy paws. His hair was plastered flat against his huge werefairy body. He was dripping, he was bedraggled, his wings were waterlogged and drooping.

And the werefairy was *not* happy. He snarled at the sea monster. He growled and he raged. Then, he started shaking. Shaking and shaking and shaking. Shaking like Bagel did after a swim in the river, shaking himself dry.

I knew. I just knew. That now, this moment, while he was shaking, *this* was our chance to escape. We *had* to take it.

And there was only one way I could think of.

'Jump,' I said to Pearl. 'JUMP!'

And we did, both of us. We jumped straight down off the rocks and on to the sea monster's back.

★ ★ ★

The sea monster shot off, with us both clinging on, arms clasped round its slippery fishy neck. It plunged away from Tide Island, powering through the water, waves of spray swooshing either side of it.

Faster and faster and faster it swam.

But not fast enough.

We heard a snarl behind us. The snarl of a werefairy, hot on the sea monster's tail.

I clung on, panicking. How long could we hang on? Who would tire first, a sea monster or a werefairy? And where was the sea monster going?

The sea monster swerved round Tide Island, straight into Lightsands Bay.

Then – disaster.

I heard the toot of a horn and the chug of an engine. I heard music. I heard laughter. Then, I saw it: a pleasure boat, a big party boat, full of lights and full of people.

And we were heading straight for it.

The sea monster swerved. It skidded right, skidded left and shuddered to a halt. I lost my grip and so did Pearl. Both of us were thrown off its back and straight up in the air . . .. which is where the werefairy swooped.

He swooped towards me as I hurtled skywards. Then, he grabbed me in his huge hairy paws. Behind me, below me, I heard a big splash: the splash of Pearl crash landing in the water. But there was no crash landing for me. I was airborne and dangling, trapped in the paws of a huge hairy werefairy.

Higher and higher we flew, above the water. I felt helpless. I felt terrified. I felt very, *very* alone.

Then, I heard something. The big town clock of Lightsands Bay was beginning to strike. Once, twice . . . seven times. And a cheer went up.

I knew what that cheer was for. The fireworks were about to begin. The fireworks. *Fireworks* . . .

Thoughts stampeded through my head: thoughts about fireworks and thoughts about Rory's dog Bagel. I remembered how Bagel hated fireworks, how he had to be shut in. How he howled and panicked. How he went crazy at the sounds and the lights. How *all* dogs did.

A feeling surged through me.

Hope.

Maybe, just maybe, it wasn't just dogs who were terrified of fireworks. Maybe wolves were too: werewolves . . . or were*fairies*.

I leaned all my weight to one side. I was going to *force* the werefairy to turn and to fly where *I* wanted: straight towards the fireworks.

Then they began.

First, a huge rocket screeched up into the sky, then exploded in a shower of thousands and thousands of tiny hot sparks. Then there were more: more and more huge fireworks, all going off, one after another.

The sky was ablaze with a dazzling display of lights and sounds. The werefairy was trembling, panicking. He didn't know which way to go. He was whimpering and quivering, and flapping about in the sky.

Then, another rocket soared straight towards us, screeching its way over the end of one huge werefairy wing. I smelt burning. I heard sizzling. The werefairy howled in pain; then he dropped me.

I plummeted.

Down and down I went, like a stone. Then, I crash landed but not in the water. I smacked down on to the tarpaulin cover of the pleasure boat. I slid down the cover and on to the deck, and landed, sprawled at the feet of two small kids sucking on lollipops.

They gaped down at me, then gaped up at the sky. Gaped up at the hairy, flapping figure with one smouldering wing. And all three of us watched the werefairy, flapping and flapping and flapping, flapping his way out to sea. We watched him disappearing into the distance, flapping like he was never *ever* going to stop.

And then, the werefairy was gone.

Chapter Thirteen

Afterwards

We made it back just in time. The grown-ups found us standing on the balcony like nothing had ever happened: no werefairy, no sea monster, nothing.

Pearl had been rescued from the water by a lady with lots of long golden hair who was out swimming.

'I was lucky she was so far out,' said Pearl. 'She pulled me to shore, then just waved and swam off again.'

'Busy doing some last-minute training for the triathlon, I expect,' I said.

Dad told me about the triathlon. It's a big one, in Lightsands, next week. A race in three parts: swimming, then cycling, then running.

'Probably,' said Pearl. 'She was a very strong swimmer.'

★ ★ ★

Talking of strong swimmers, that sea monster and all those attacks, that swerving through the water, smacking its tailfin down, I reckon they were all aimed at Harry. Maybe a monster can spot other monsters. Maybe it doesn't like other monsters being in its territory.

It certainly seemed harmless to humans. Maybe it wasn't really a monster at all, not on the inside.

Unlike Harry.

I had a *lot* of questions about Harry. Where did he come from? Why was he here? Where did he go? Were there *more* werefairies out there or just Harry?

I'll never know the answer to those questions but I don't mind, because one thing I *do* know. Battling a werefairy is a good way for two kids to become friends. And, back home, I've made a new den: a better one, with Pearl. When Rory comes to visit – happening soon – we'll show him. I reckon he'll like it.

As for Pearl, she was three, maybe four, when she saw her monster. It was a giant slug thing with big purple pincers. It slithered into next door's garden and ate their Chihuahua.

'Mum and Dad told me it was a dream,' Pearl said. 'But I always thought it was weird that the dog went missing the morning after my dream.'

Now she knew why.

★ ★ ★

Magnus wasn't too sad about Harry being gone because he found a note tucked under his pillow.

Dear Magnus,
Thank you for being my friend.
I have to leave you, because I have a very important new job. I am now tooth fairy to some royal babies.

Harry

Fifteen whole minutes it took me to decide what kind of handwriting a fairy would have.

Magnus was thrilled. 'A note!' he said, clasping his hands. 'I must take a picture of my note for Fairy Fenella!'

★ ★ ★

Mum turned up the next day and I knew straight away that Dad had been talking to her, telling her how I scared Magnus about monsters and pretended to see things through the binoculars. When Mum asked me to show her the cliff path, I knew she was planning a chat with me.

She was. As we stood at the top of the cliff path, Mum spoke. 'Stan,' she said. 'About monsters . . . all this pretending . . .'

She stopped. She stood still. She stared out to sea and went pale. 'Oh my goodness,' she said.

I knew why. The sea monster was out there, basking, right next to Tide Island. It was floating on its back, worn out by yesterday. It had stretched itself out on the surface, frills flopping all around its head.

I could see it, clear as clear and, I realised, so could Mum. She blinked and shook her head. We walked on and the chat was over.

★ ★ ★

Magnus and Claudia never spotted the sea monster but they did spot something else.

I was building a theme park for gorillas in the sand with Pearl when I heard thudding behind me. I turned and saw Claudia and Magnus thudding across the sand.

'Princess Splishy-Splashy,' bellowed Claudia, pointing. 'Look. Look! She's back!'

So we looked and there she was, sitting out on the rocks of Tide Island and combing her long golden hair. A mermaid, who gave us all a friendly wave.

Pearl took one look and her jaw dropped. 'Her,' she said. 'It was her! *She* was the swimmer. She was the one who rescued me.'

Just then, Mum came out of Shiversands Cottage. 'Lunch is ready,' she said. She stopped and gaped at the rocks of Tide Island, at Princess Splishy-Splashy, sitting there, waving. She rubbed her eyes and went back inside.

Poor Mum.

Maybe I'll explain to her one day, explain that the dream she had, the one that seemed so real to her when she was small, *was* real. Maybe I'll explain that she's got magic eyes.

Or maybe not. I doubt she'd believe me.

* * *

As for magic eyes, it doesn't seem to matter what you see first: a fairy, a monster, a mermaid. Once you've seen one magical creature, you can see them all.

So I'm keeping my eyes peeled.

Maybe there are goblins on our planet. Real ones.

You never know.